AF447478

THAT ONE EXTRA LIE

Aurélien Gilbert

THAT ONE
EXTRA LIE

Translated from the French by

Andrew Starr

ISBN 979-10-94170-03-8

Dépôt légal: septembre 2015
© Aurélien Gilbert, 2015
Maisons-Laffitte, France

© English version: Andrew Starr, 2015
© Original French version: Aurélien Gilbert, 2014

I

"Louis, are you ready? We'll be late!"

"Very funny! You've been hogging the bathroom for a whole hour now."

I used my most convincing tone. In all honesty, her make-up session had allowed me to finish the end of my TV programme in peace.

Delphine glanced through the half-open doorway.

"Oh, I see did you need the wash basin to help you put your trousers on?"

She always had to have the last word. I didn't blame her, being able to give a quick comeback was a necessary gift in her career. Delphine was a Biology teacher, she taught in a high school in Biarritz where she had undertaken some of her own schooling. A native of Lyon, I had joined her two years ago, and we moved in together. We were not exactly rolling in money then, so we'd gone for the best compromise between the right geographical position and a reasonably sized living space. We eventually fell for the charms of a flat right in the centre of town, a stone's throw from the shops and the sea. With a little more space, it would have been considered luxurious. However, to keep to our tight budget we were resigned to a simple but functional studio flat rather than the two-bed flat we'd so wanted. It consisted of a multi-function room and a tiny room intended to be a bathroom and toilet. It could be said that this room, lacking a bathtub was hardly what you would call a convenience, let alone a bathroom, except perhaps if you were a contortionist.

We were lucky to have quite high ceilings in the main room, so I built a wooden mezzanine floor by myself to allow us to get a few extra square metres of space. We kept our bed up there, underneath was an office, partitioned off by glass, where you could sit without having to keep your head down. Delphine would happily do her marking there while I watched the TV next to her. Don't get me wrong, the DIY and decorating programmes I watched were strictly for my job as an interior designer.

Summer had just begun. The evenings were warm and the town basked in orange-tinted light. That Friday we'd been invited to dinner at Alice and Maxime's house, a couple of friends, who lived in a neighbouring part of town, about a fifteen-minute stroll away. This time we really had to get a move on. When we left, we were already half an hour late, so Delphine took the lead with little steps and I strode after her. On the way, our pace was so focussed that we didn't dare exchange a word in case it broke our concentration. It was far from easy; we had to decide between the optimum speed and arriving with an acceptable amount of sweat on us. The warm and moist air wasn't exactly helping either.

"Just eight minutes to get here, we've saved the day!" I panted at Delphine once we were in front of the flats.

Delphine punched in the passcode, and then we went up to the third floor. Alice opened the door to us.

"Hi, Delphine. What news since last night? Louis, it's been a long time! Come in, Maxime has made cocktails for you both."

Maxime appeared with a glass in each hand, it wasn't so easy for me to get one from him. As usual, he'd made us his Long Island Iced Tea using his own special measures.

"Sit down, you're dripping with sweat, you been running or what?" I let Delphine explain our countless reasons for being late while I made myself comfortable on the sofa.

Alice and Maxime were not your average couple. Alice was a tall brown-haired woman who knew how to get the best from life while Maxime, much shorter than her, got himself noticed due to his loud mouth and legendary ability to boast. Some say that opposites attract, while others will have it that birds of a feather flock together. Endless arguments follow that sometimes lead to blows.

To come back to Alice and Maxime for a moment, although, at first sight, you would think they were a mismatched pair, their union was born of their common passion, medicine. They'd spent long years studying together in Bordeaux after which they'd married and each opened their own surgery in Biarritz.

Alice was a psychiatrist and her husband a dermatologist. Alice and Delphine's paths had crossed even earlier in their schooling, at Primary School in Biarritz. The two friends had never lost contact and currently visited each other every Thursday. Alice probably knew much more about Delphine than I did and conversely Delphine has told me some stories about Alice that poor Maxime was a long way from ever being able to contemplate.

It was Maxime who roused me from my daydreaming by shaking a packet of peanuts under my nose.

"So Louis, how's work going?"

"Work? Don't talk to me about work! On Monday, a customer asked me to renovate his living room in the style of a Romanesque villa. I spent the whole week working on sourcing statues, columns and mosaics. This morning I presented the project to him. The pratt responds by telling me that it's out of the question that his Norman wardrobes, which take up more than half the room are to be moved out! I ought to have just slapped two or three amphorae in a corner that would have been better for all concerned. At the end of the day, that's all part of the job. It's got to cross your mind sometimes to want to bump your clients off with your scalpel."

"You mean my patients? On the contrary, they're much more use to me alive." Maxime contradicted me while waving his new watch at me. "Look at this! At the age of 33, I thought it was about time I got myself a Rolex. Recently, there's been a swarm of jellyfish at Biarritz and that's just manna from heaven for the business. So as you can see I'm living for the moment. The one thing worrying me about the near future, though, is the growing efficiency of acne creams; the whole market is going to collapse. Sadly, I'm no longer of the opinion that there'll be enough new skin complaints coming along that'll allow the market to grow again. Alice goes nuts when she hears me talking like this, but you know, the human body is a business, just like any other. Talking of her, where have the girls got to? Gabbing about clothes probably?"

"We're in the kitchen, Delphine is explaining to me how mitochondria work." Alice retorted from the neighbouring room. "Just so you know, we can hear all your nonsense."

Maxime winked at me: "The main course will be here soon. Alice has made a Norwegian style burbot stew, but it was me who cooked the rice that goes with it!"

Once everyone was seated around the table, the conversation took a dangerous political turn, starting with a debate about speed cameras.

"I got flashed last night on the way to meet Delphine. I wasn't careful enough," confessed Alice.

"You fall into their traps, they try to make you feel guilty by making you believe that the money they are stealing from you is theirs by right." Maxime revealed to her in such a way you'd almost believe he knew what he was talking about.

"Where were you going anyway?"

"To the Table à Cinq Pieds."

The Table à Cinq Pieds was a restaurant on the seafront, which had the peculiarity of paying homage to the number five with all its furnishings and equipment. Its plates were pentagonal, the tables and chairs alike were equipped with five legs, the forks had five prongs, and five armed chandeliers lighted all.

It was this revelation from Alice that seemed most odd to me.

"You ate at the Table à Cinq Pieds?" I asked again, even though it made me look stupid.

"Exactly," said Delphine. "I had the lamb in the five herb sauce as usual, lovely."

You could have heard a pin drop at that point.

"Right, if you don't mind, I think I'll fetch that dessert Delphine brought." Alice finally announced.

Everyone congratulated Delphine on her orange drizzle cake while I lost myself in much darker thoughts.

"Louis, is everything alright?"

"I'm bushed. I think all these late nights are catching up with me. I can hear my bed calling me."

"Looking at those bags under your eyes, you'd be best off going to bed," Maxime advised me. "And that's a doctor speaking here! Alice can tell you her crazy stories next time."

On the way home, I kept my teeth clenched. Delphine tried to break the silence. "What did you think of my orange drizzle cake?"

"Bitter, far too bitter."

For a reason I did not yet know, Alice and Delphine had lied. During the week, I had passed by the Table à Cinq Pieds to get to a customer's house. That restaurant was closed for building work.

II

I tossed and turned in bed, so much so that I got tangled up in the sheets, all the while Delphine slept deeply and soundly. Questions were getting mixed up in my mind, one question led to another. What reason could Delphine possibly have had to lie to me about her schedule? She'd always been so honest with me, sometimes too honest. The last time was when I'd bought her a handbag, after spending a long time choosing which brand. With absolutely no thought for my feelings, she told me that it wasn't to her liking and she went off to exchange it that very same day.

I also didn't understand how she could've involved Alice in her lies; she was in my eyes kindness incarnate. As for Maxime, had he also betrayed me just like Judas? What if he was the husband who was being cheated on? If this were so, then Delphine would've lied to cover for Alice. Just thinking about that raised a smile on my face despite my sour mood. However, I soon sank back down into the seriousness of the situation, realising that it still didn't explain what had happened with Delphine the evening before.

Another idea eased my pain a little. The three of them could've had a secret meeting to organise a surprise for me. Admittedly I'd celebrated my birthday last month, but Alice and Maxime were away on holiday so couldn't be there on the day.

I'd gone over repeatedly in my mind the events of the previous days; nothing out of the ordinary had allowed me to come down more in favour of any one of my ideas. I had definitely noticed Delphine had been more stressed than normal. Her last two year-end class meetings had been rough, there were definitely some raised voices when it was mentioned that particular pupils would have to repeat the year. As she'd been on holiday since yesterday, she'd soon be a long way from all that stress.

My need, to get to the bottom of this unusual situation had reached crisis point. I had to be more practical. With this aim in mind, the easiest solution would be to ask Delphine directly. I was not going to do that of course. By reacting like that, all I would achieve would be to rouse her suspicions, losing any possibility of finding the real answer to my questions.

A much better way of working did come to mind: looking at her mobile phone to see whom she'd contacted over the last few days. This would raise an ethical problem, but I'd have to overlook it. I found myself in a situation completely beyond my control. After all some governments out there, have no problems getting such information. So why should I worry about it any longer?

I began the quest for the phone straight away. Sitting on the bed up in the mezzanine I had a view across the whole room. The town's lights were coming through the curtains, allowing me to make out Delphine's iPhone through the darkness down there on the table. Next to me, its owner seemed to be sleeping like a baby. I tried to go down the steps, but when I reached the middle of the ladder my foot slipped and one of the rungs creaked. Delphine groaned in her sleep, clinging on to the post I held my breath.

"Louis, what're you doing?" Delphine asked me sleepily.

"I'm getting a glass of water." I thought my quick response there was impressive, a simple but reasonably quick on the draw answer. I began climbing the ladder again, then I realised that just as it should be in politics a little bit of putting words into action would not go amiss. For appearance's sake, I went back down again to get a drink and decided that I'd start the quest again tomorrow because it was just too risky now.

Delphine woke me up whistling a tune accompanied by birdsong. She'd opened the curtains and from the bed I was able to look at the sea sparkling under a cloudless sky. The delicate aroma of coffee and crois-sants caught my nose telling me that she'd been up a while. It was obvious that my mood had totally changed in the space of a few hours. I've no idea what could've got into me, to be worrying half the night like that instead of getting a good night's sleep? I'd so often do this when I worried about work late into the night. Usually, the ideas that had kept me up and I'd thought so brilliant the night before would somehow lose their shine once I'd woken up.

After a few more moments of sleepy bliss, I got a hold of myself by thinking about the mobile phone.

Among all my pointless thoughts, this one came to the fore. It gave me the reason to get up I was waiting for.

"It sure looks like you've slept well," Delphine said to me, "It's almost 11 o'clock!" Her tone was perky; she seemed to have put that yesterday's mood of mine down to tiredness.

"Thanks for the croissants, they're just what I needed."

While waiting for the truth to come out, I thought it best to be better company than I'd been the night before. After all, just like everyone else, Delphine had the right to be presumed innocent until proven guilty.

"I'll leave you to it, I'm going for a shower," she announced after a while. A few moments later I heard the water hitting the sides of the shower cubicle. I hurried to Delphine's iPhone. In the list of received, made and missed calls over the last two days there was her Maths teacher colleague Laeticia, her brother Julien, her friend Alice and me. At first sight, there was nothing untoward. Looking through the text messages, there was just one, which caught my attention. It came from someone named "Dimitri School" unknown number and had as its contents "I can't come to the PS2 class meeting, please tell Bernardeau x". Unless it had been written in an extremely elaborate code, this message was definitely not one to worry about. Looking through her Internet search history I found stuff, which would bore me to tears. "Date summer sales", "Calories in kouign-amann", "Recipe orange drizzle cake" as well as around 10 more just like those. Obviously Delphine had thought of everything. She must've meticulously erased any compromising information.

I'd begun to lose hope when I had a brainwave. What about the GPS app? Bingo! The day before Delphine had looked up the route from Biarritz to Aïnhoa.

This little discovery allowed me to know her exact destination. Her uncle had a little shepherd's house in the countryside not far from Aïnhoa village.

This uncle had moved into a retirement complex a few years before. He'd given his keys to Delphine, who was the only family member he still had living in the area. We'd been there several times and I thought I'd easily be able to find the way there from the village. I just had to find the best time to organise my little escapade.

That very afternoon there was a golden opportunity. Delphine had been curiously overcome by an irresistible desire to go shopping. This could easily be explained by the beginning of her holidays coinciding with the start of the summer sales, a particularly lethal cocktail. This frenzy seems very alien to me though I never said I was above the charms of mass consumption. In fact, it is an important part of my job. However constantly trying things on and queuing at tills doesn't fill me with any more glee than pushing a trolley around a supermarket does. This, however, doesn't stop me enjoying having a well-stocked fridge or a newly purchased suit.

Delphine asked me to go with her, just because she felt she ought. In the past, I'd all too often accepted this offer by mistake and we both ended up regretting it. When I declined her offer, just as she'd hoped I would, she was off like a shot.

Fidgeting with impatience, I ferreted in vain around every corner of the house, looking for the keys to that house in Aïnhoa, which weren't where they should be. I'd have to just make do without them. I took the trouble to write a little note explaining I had gone off somewhere and I hurried off towards the car park, where my sporty little car awaited, a red Clio. It took me a good half hour to reach the village. After I'd crossed the dirt track, I remembered it. The last time I'd used it went back to the previous summer when we'd got up early to go on a long walk across the mountain. I really liked this place and I wasn't alone in that. Its reputation attracts tourists and ramblers alike who criss-cross the village as much as they do its surroundings. It's purely by luck that the area remains so remarkably well pre-served. After just a few minutes' walk, you can find yourself surrounded by nature, with amazing views encompassing a large part of the locality from the Pyrenees to the Atlantic.

Once I could see the house, I parked the car out of view. My car's vibrant red colour wouldn't go unno-ticed. Stepping out of the air-conditioned compartment I realised that the heat outside had become unbearable. I'd gone a few metres towards the house when I noticed that the front door seemed to be slightly open. I wasn't that worried that there might have been a burglary; the old stone house had nothing of great value in it. From the outside, I couldn't detect any noise. After a few minutes observation I decided to go in, I just had to push gently on the door for it to open. I remained for a moment on the threshold, while my eyes got used to the darkness inside. Suddenly I was overcome with fear. There was a man, just there lying on the bed.

III

"Louis? What on Earth are you doing here?"

"Julien! But why are you here?"

Julien was Delphine's younger brother, he lived somewhere in Paris and I'd never have expected to find him here. I'd seen a call from Julien on Delphine's phone a few hours earlier, but I'd dismissed it as soon as I'd seen it. Julien had left Biarritz for Paris because he found it too small and not lively enough for his tastes. The quiet and fresh air made his stomach turn. Finding him in this isolated house was a bit like him surprising me sitting in a deck chair on top of a hideously urban concrete slab.

Julien quickly brought me back down to Earth.

"Did my sister tell you to come poking around here?" he suddenly growled. Judging by his aggressive yet sluggish tone, I'd probably woken him.

"Not at all, she doesn't even know I'm here. How are things with you anyway?"

"Are you taking the mick? Get out of here!"

"Oh well, that's nice! What's wrong with you?"

Julien was now upright on his bed, looming. The room was shrouded in darkness; the thick stonewalls were of an almost icy coldness, contrasting sharply with the outside heat.

I hesitated for a moment, caught between hightailing it out of there and having the courage to remain. First of all I decided to use all the moves I had learned to calm an overexcited dog. Avoiding any sudden movement, I brought a chair slowly towards me. To my surprise, Julien seemed to understand I just wanted to calmly talk and there was no need to bite. He calmly sat himself down and told me the reasons, which had made him flee the capital.

Julien had moved to Paris a little over a year ago. Over time, he'd found himself a job waiting on tables and met a neighbour of his, Elsa, who worked in a nearby souvenir shop and lived at the bottom of his block of flats. The two lovebirds seemed made for each other. Elsa wasted no time moving in with him.

The darkness in the room was beginning to get to me. "Sorry to stop you, but I'm just going to open the shutters. You can't see a thing in here!"

In the daylight, I noticed that Julien looked really unkempt. He was scruffy, unshaven and had drawn out features. Although his story had a wonderful beginning, I wouldn't be betting on a happy end.

Julien continued with his story, he took us back four days. As a couple, they were celebrating their first anniversary of moving in together. Julien made the most of the occasion by asking Elsa to marry him and she'd said yes straight away.

The euphoria, however, was short-lived. Elsa hadn't come home from work by dinnertime the following day. Being very worried, he'd tried calling her the whole evening and had called her parents and friends. No one could give him any news of her whatsoever.

After a sleepless night, he finally received a text message. The message was concise and unambiguous: "I'm leaving you" Julien was left reeling, why make such a decision when all was going so well? Was his marriage proposal too premature? Had Elsa perhaps panicked?

He'd tried again unsuccessfully to call her. He'd then hurried to the shop where she worked, just below his flat; she wasn't there either.

Julien was crushed. In the brasserie, his boss soon realised he wasn't right and advised him to take a few days leave to escape from it all. I came to the conclusion that I too would have taken the same initiative faced with an employee who looked like the guy I had here in front of me. Just the way he looked was enough to make any customers run away screaming.

Following his boss' good advice, he'd decided to hole up here in his uncle's house. Just this once he wanted to be alone, but once he'd arrived at Biarritz station, he realised he'd have to go to his sister's place to fetch the keys. He'd called her and went to wait for her at the school gates.

"Delphine came here with you?"

"Yes, it was her who brought me here. As I had no food in, we did some shopping. After that, I'll admit I went a bit too far. I told her to get lost and that she should just leave me in peace. I just wanted to take it easy, but it seems she took it badly.

"You don't say!"

Delphine must have been really annoyed. I'd had the misfortune of upsetting her for much less than that.

Whenever I did, it was always best to keep a low profile and avoid at all costs going back to the original reason for the upset. It was probably because of this that Delphine had chosen to keep silent. Alice was the only person in whom she would have been able to confide such a humiliation. As the two of them should have been meeting up that same evening, they must have both decided to hush the whole thing up, without giving a thought to me being such an astute detective.

I felt ashamed for having ever doubted Delphine. Besides, the amazing story her brother had just told me was absolutely none of my business. Feeling a little ill at ease, I decided to take my leave and return to Biarritz.

"Say hi to Delphine for me, but just so there's no confusion, I really don't need her here. I don't want to see either of you here again." Julien made his feelings clear while firmly shaking my hand.

I took the little path that led back to my car and got back on the road to Biarritz. On the way, I mulled over how I was going to present things to Delphine. It was best to tell her everything now, rather than making a serious mistake by allowing it to descend into a web of lies.

On my arrival, I realised that Delphine had returned from her shopping. Bags were strewn all around the entrance to the flat. I sat down opposite her and told her everything. Relieved that the truth was out Delphine didn't take umbrage, at least for the moment, over my solo adventure. She made it clear that her brother's attitude towards her had really upset her. The last time she'd seen him, he was in such a foul mood from start to finish. She was over it though and the lad's mood swings would pass over her head from now on. I explained to her that Julien really didn't intend to upset her, but that he was deep in the depths of despair and wanted to be alone. Delphine was really shocked to hear that Elsa had left her brother. Julien hadn't even mentioned this fact.

I thought long and hard about the lie she had told, about the restaurant. I came to the conclusion that no matter how strong blood and marriage ties are, sometimes it's easier to confide in friends or brothers-in-law than to confide in your partner or your brothers and sisters.

Delphine confirmed that she had indeed made up the alibi with Alice, as she was worried that I'd make things worse once I learned how rude her brother had been to her. Alice had ended up having dinner at another friend's house. As for Maxime, he was such a blabbermouth that Alice had carefully avoided talking to him about that evening at all.

I'd also passed quickly over the catalyst for my trip out and Delphine knew just how to remind me of that:

"So you'd rather have gone through my phone than to talk to me about it?"

"And you'd rather have lied about your whereabouts than talk to me about it?"

I'd prepared this comeback ready on the way back.

"It was none of your business. My iPhone, on the other hand, that is my business."

I hadn't expected this response and didn't know how best to answer. Never mind, the matter was closed. I'd skilfully change the subject by begging Delphine to show me her new purchases. A little diplomacy never did anyone any harm.

She made me look at all her new clothes, her new dresses, slipovers and little tops. In the wake of all this she suggested we should go for a run on the beach, to make the most of the early evening. We tried to do something sporty at least once a week. A minimal amount so we can benefit from the feeling of doing something to alleviate our consciences. When it's too cold, we swim instead of running.

I put my heart rate monitor on, along with my jogging bottoms and running shoes and I was ready to go. As was our habit, we began by going down towards the beach, before running along the sea where the wet sand meets the dry. The sun had begun to set, but it was still powerfully hot. Delphine remained lost in her thoughts. Her brother's retreat into his shell was really worrying her. She brought the burning issue up again.

"Do you think he's started getting over the break-up?"

"Not at all, I think he's more likely going into a depression."

If she was looking for reassurance from me, she wasn't going to get it.

"It's all really worrying, we should go back to talk to him."

"That's a really bad idea, he told me repeatedly, and even half threatened me that he was to be left alone. If we go back there, it'll most likely end badly."

"I've another solution!" declared Delphine after a moment's reflection. "As I'm now on holiday, I'd really like to go do a spot of touring around Paris. I'll use this time to talk to this Elsa. It's really odd how she just disappeared like that without any explanation."

"Why not, in that case, I'll take a few days off myself and come with you."

IV

I'd been working in Biarritz for several years now. A short while after my arrival, I'd taken on the customers of an interior designer who'd recently retired and with whom I'd started my career. Business was pretty good. In this area, there was no shortage of customers wishing to give their villas a makeover. Luckily, for me they didn't seem to be suffering too much from the financial crisis. During the first few years, I systematically took every job, which came my way. My bookings took off so much that my days off became fewer and fewer. I ended up by understanding that once I was honouring enough contracts, I could allow myself to refuse a few, especially those, which came from customers whose tastes, were particularly dubious. From that moment on, I was able to use my time as I saw fit. This allowed me to give myself a few days off at short notice that week so I could go to Paris with Delphine.

We took the train early on Tuesday morning and got off at Montparnasse station around midday. Delphine suggested that we took line number 12 to make our way to Julien's high-rise, at the foot of which stood the little shop where Elsa worked. That day, I discovered the delights of Parisian underground trains during heat waves. Following an incident due to "Passenger illness", we found ourselves in a packed train. It was so full that an accordionist who was waiting on the platform with us decided to wait for the next one to make his journey. Trapped under the armpit of an imposing gentleman who very obviously not yet discovered the wonders of soap, my nostrils were attacked by a wide variety of unusual odours with bitter undertones of an intensely musky base, causing my eyes and throat to sting.

Paris is without a doubt a wonderful city, but she can so quickly become oppressive. On the other hand, Parisians would probably see Biarritz as a pleasant town in which to spend the summer holidays, but truly depressing in the long winter months. For me, the months of July and August were exactly the worst ones in Biarritz, during which the sound of waves crashing on the shore are almost imperceptible over the noise of the hundreds of holidaymakers. Seeing the advancing hordes of Parisians every summer armed with their buckets, spades and duck shaped life rings, I long for my deserted and ice cool wintry beach.

We left the Paris Underground at Lamarck-Caulaincourt station, which isn't far from the Sacré Coeur and Montmartre. Delphine led us to her brother's address. As expected there was a small souvenir shop occupying the ground floor, we went in.

It was one of those places that sold things, which can be sorted into two main categories: things to make people think of Paris and things made in China. The only exceptions to this rule were shortbread biscuits from Mont St Michel hidden in a corner.

I wondered how such a business could survive on this little street away from the main crowds. There was nobody there apart from the saleswoman who was busy chatting on the phone to some unknown person. She was slumped behind the till, moaning one minute about the heat, the next about her husband. Underneath her thick layer of foundation, I'd say she was well into her fifties. Hoping that she'd cut her phone conversation short, we went round the shop, making out we were really interested in the quality of the glass beads on display. Nothing worked though. That bad-mannered woman barely even glanced in our direction. When she finally did hang up, Delphine instantly put the Sacré Coeur snow globe she was examining down and hurried off towards her.

"Hello, Could I please speak to Elsa?"

"Oh, her!"

"Yes is she here?"

"No!"

"So do you know where she is?"

"No idea!"

"We must speak to her, it's really important."

The saleswoman nonchalantly eyed each of us up in turn.

"Right, I'll fetch Paul."

Seemingly, out of the kindness of her heart, she made a huge effort to get up out of her chair and disappeared into the backroom.

I went up to Delphine. "Wow, what a warm welcome. If I ever decide to buy an Eiffel Tower key ring, it definitely won't be from here!"

A very tall and slim young man came out of the backroom beaming from ear to ear. Before he had even opened his mouth, he'd made up for the terrible impression his colleague had made on us.

"Hello sir, madam, Paul at your service. Marthe told me that you were looking for Elsa?"

"Yes we'd like to talk to her, do you know where she is?" Delphine asked.

"If it's not too bold a question, are you family or friends?"

"Neither, I'm her boyfriend's sister."

"Oh, I see! She's your brother's girlfriend. I'm really sorry, but she hasn't been here for days. She sent a text to warn us that she wouldn't be coming in. She went to stay with a cousin somewhere in the country. She needed some time out to think things over. I should say that the day before she left, she was all over the place here in the shop, she'd had a row with your brother and they'd broken up."

"They'd argued?" Delphine sounded shocked.

"Yes and if I'm not mistaken, she must've left after she'd finished work. The next day your brother came in here first thing and practically turned half the shop upside down looking for her. He even went in the back, we nearly called the police."

"I'm very sorry for my brother, he's not usually like that. He must have been suffering from the shock of it all."

"Oh no, I'm really sorry. Julien used to come here from time to time. They really seemed to have hit it off. It's such a shame that it ended so badly."

We left even more confused than we were before. Julien had never mentioned any argument having taken place before he received that break-up text message. What possible reason could he have had to bend the truth like that?

He did not even have to tell me that his marriage proposal had been so well received.

Once outside we passed through the gated entrance adjoining the shop so we would have a look at Julien's Block. We came out into a little yard, on the other side of which a staircase led off to different flats. A man appeared out of nowhere and came up to us, introducing himself as the flat's caretaker. His face lit up as Delphine said her brother's name.

Being a friendly caretaker, he told us energetically of all Elsa and Julien's comings and goings. Julien had come to see him in a real state last week, asking if he had seen Elsa at all. Not only had he not seen her at that time, but also she'd not been back to her own flat either, so she'd left all her stuff there. The shutters remained closed and the letterbox was overflowing with mail. According to our storyteller, something really bad must have happened.

He'd said all this to Elsa's parents, who were also unable to contact her. I told him what we'd learned from the shop employee, that Elsa had left a few days ago to go to her cousin's house. The caretaker was ready to talk some more, but the afternoon was wearing on and we were really beginning to feel hungry. He gave us the address of the brasserie where Julien worked, which was just a few streets away. It wasn't a bad idea, as I was itching to get out and see a bit more of the city.

Despite the fact that it was already quite late, the brasserie was still open for lunch. We sat ourselves down at the tables out the front so we could make the most of the sun. Delphine ordered a cheeseburger. I said to her that it was hardly a local speciality, but then I could barely name anything particularly Parisian myself.

While waiting for the meals, we had a chance to talk to Julien's boss. He did not know much about it, except that Elsa's parents had called the Brasserie several times over the past few days. They were going crazy over the caretaker's very macabre theories about what might have happened to her.

During dessert, Delphine's phone rang. The number began with 01, which meant it had originated in Paris. As she answered, I got stuck into my profiteroles because I was worried that the melted chocolate might heat the ice cream, or that ice cream might cool the melted chocolate. I was only half listening to the conversation until Delphine put her hand over the microphone and whispered to me, as white as a sheet:

"It's the police station. Elsa's parents have initiated a missing person's investigation."

V

Delphine and the police superintendent spoke for a while on the phone. The police, not being able to get hold of Julien had ended up contacting Delphine. She wasted no time telling them the Aïnhoa address so that a team of police from Espelette, the neighbouring village, could be sent to find her brother as soon as possible. A meeting was immediately arranged at the police station a few stops by underground train from where we were so that everything we knew could be told to the police to help the inquiry move forward.

When we arrived, a small, serious looking bespectacled man came to meet us. His salt and pepper coloured goatee gave him, to my mind, an investigative appearance.

"I'm Superintendent Colin, pleased to meet you! I spoke to you just now on the phone." The superintendent took us to his office, a large room whose decor looked like something out of the sixties. The beige lino went so well with the brownish wall covering and the Formica table really complimented the metallic cupboards. The highly modern computer, even more modern than mine took pride of place on the desk and seemed so out of keeping with the rest of the room.

The superintendent showed us to two fake leather chairs and turned towards Delphine.

"Before we get started, do you have a recent photo of your brother you could e-mail to me? To put you in the picture, it seems that any photos we have of him are very out-dated, he looks about twelve in them."

Delphine hesitated for a moment, worried that she would be betraying her brother. However, Julien was obviously innocent so there seemed no reason to put any obstacles in the way of the police investigation.

"Yes, there are some at home in Biarritz... But a friend of mine has photos of our wedding and he must be in some of them. Looking at the time, she must be home by now. I'll just go and call her and I'll come back."

I knew that the friend in question must be Alice. After a few minutes, Delphine reappeared from the neighbouring room.

"My friend is going to send us the photos of Julien, we'll be able to get them on your computer soon."

The superintendent kept his serious expression, looking thoughtfully at us through knitted eyebrows:

"Right let me get you up to speed with the situation. Elsa's parents have been in to see us to express their concern about their daughter. They gave us a range of evidence that has allowed us to take her disappearance seriously. To put you in the picture, the prosecutor has begun enquiries today into this worrying disappearance. It is now one week since anyone has seen or heard from the young woman. She has taken none of her things with her and there has been no activity on her bank account since the date she went missing. To put you in the picture, we can't rule out either kidnapping or murder at this moment in time."

On hearing these words, I felt Delphine shake next to me. The superintendent continued: "The problem is that we have until now, been unable to locate your brother Julien, who is best placed to fill in the details. You told me just now that you've seen him recently, so tell me about it."

Delphine went into broad details about our respective visits to Aïnhoa. Once the superintendent understood that our presence in Paris was not just coincidental, he seemed taken aback. Obviously thinking that we too suspected Julien, he began to accuse him openly. I decided to intervene: "With no evidence to the contrary, we believe that Julien has done nothing wrong. If he can't be reached, it's because his mobile is out of signal range where he is. I had the same problem with my own phone when I went to see him there. Julien went there to clear his head and he'll be able to explain all this to your colleagues in a few minutes. What's more, I don't see what's so worrying about this disappearance. Elsa had even sent a break-up text message through to him along with one to her colleague stating that she was staying with her cousin."

"I know nothing about these text messages," the superintendent stated. "To put you in the picture, we're still waiting for the detailed version of Elsa's phone bill. Don't you think her parents would have spoken to her friends and family? This story of her cousin seems a bit off to me. It is highly likely that another person could have sent these texts from Elsa's phone. Rest assured, we'll check all this information with the family and for all you…"

A terribly loud ringing noise interrupted him. I thought it was perhaps a fire alarm or a bomb alert. It was just the telephone. The conversation barely lasted 30 seconds. As he replaced the receiver, the superintendent nervously stroked his goatee between his thumb and forefinger.

"That was the police in Espelette. They found nobody at the Aïnhoa house. Your brother has got away from us, taking all his things with him."

A shiver went down my spine. I had to take a good look at all the evidence. The superintendent had been correct right from the start. The expression that Julien had used "to escape from it all" in front of me now made perfect sense, he was on the run.

If we just stick to the two lines of inquiry, the superintendent had given us: kidnap and murder, the first was fairly unlikely. Delphine and I had both driven and seen Julien alone. As for the idea of murder, that had never entered my head, until now.

Several different elements had played their part in our self-deception. The text messages, which Julien could have in all truth sent himself from Elsa's phone and above all the story he'd told me which I had never doubted for one moment.

As for murder, I could imagine nothing other than an accident, doubtlessly caused by an argument. Which lead to the lie about what caused the argument that broke them up, the same lie that Elsa's colleague must have heard about. I'd witnessed with my own eyes how impulsive Julien's nature could be.

Once he'd disposed of the body. Julien would've quickly realised that the house in Aïnhoa would've made an excellent bolthole for someone on the run than anywhere in the Paris region, particularly because of its proximity to Spain. As both Delphine and I knew where he was staying, he wouldn't be able to prolong his stay.

As Julien was not expert at being on the run, the superintendent was hoping to find him quickly. If he took any money out at a cash machine or switched his mobile back on again, the police would easily be able to locate him.

Before we left, Delphine explained how to get the photos Alice had sent to us. Superintendent Colin gave us his card and told us to call him should Julien ever show up.

The return trip to Biarritz was depressing. The following day I spent the whole afternoon on the Romanesque style lounge project I was working on so I could clear my head a little. Delphine went off to her uncle's house in the little hope that she could find any clue that would lead her to her brother. It would be in vain. On the other hand, we had no more news from Superintendent Colin either, who'd promised us, in his own words, to let us know if there were any developments on his side.

That evening, Delphine had invited Alice and Maxime to dinner. This was a good thing as they'd be able to look at everything from a new perspective. We'd organised a simple meal, made up of home delivered pizzas. While I laid the foldable table, someone rang the doorbell.

"That'll be the pizzas, can you go?" Delphine went to open the door. It wasn't the pizzas or our guests. It was Julien.

VI

We weren't prepared for this sudden arrival. Julien must've realised that he couldn't last long on the run and had probably decided to come and ask us for money.

"What brings you here?" Delphine asked him, trying to appear as normal as possible. There was no way we'd be letting him leave now.

"I'd had enough of being holed up in that old shack; I decided to go off the beaten track and slept under the stars last night. I thought I'd just stop by before going back up to Paris."

Delphine was able to gain his trust, listening to her; he'd have had absolutely no idea he was actively sought after. Without knowing it, he'd climbed into the trap, which was to ensnare him.

"Oh, that's really nice of you, you… Ah, there's the doorbell. It must be Alice and Maxime."

"Oh I'm being a nuisance, I'll go!" Julien said.

"Hey Ju, don't leave me hanging here! You'll at least have dinner with us won't you?"

The situation was becoming extremely difficult. Delphine had already brought Alice up to date about our little adventure to Paris and of our suspicions about Julien. There'd have to be no slip-ups. The major blunderer among us was without a shadow of doubt Maxime. I quickly took him off to one side into the bathroom under the pretext of an issue with the cistern and wanting to make use of his boundless plumbing capabilities. I quickly put him in the picture. Delphine, for her part, was able to communicate everything to Alice through glances and nodding. The pizza delivery guy decided he was going to turn up right in the middle of all this. As for Julien, he seemed unaware that anything was up.

Once the pre-dinner drinks were sorted, I instigated an urgent call to a customer so that I could warn Superintendent Colin as quickly as possible of Julien's presence. Delphine screwed her eyes up to give me the go-ahead. I positioned myself in the little office area under the mezzanine barely a few metres from the table. The acoustics under there were enough to enable me to make a phone call using a low voice and the glass partition allowed me to see what was happening on the other side. I took the superintendent's card out of my pocket and I dialled the number.

"Good evening, I…"

"Ah Good evening young man, you've called at just the right time, I was about to call you." interrupted the superintendent.

"Julien is here with us. He doesn't suspect a thing, but we can't keep him here for long." I whispered.

"Well we've some news, we've just found Elsa!"

"Oh really? How is she?" I was expecting the worst.

"Rest assured she's fine, her aggressor, on the other hand, is likely to spend quite some time behind bars, to put you in the picture."

"It would seem like the inquiry was reaching its end." The superintendent's voice was hardly recognisable he seemed so relaxed. However, what he'd just told me brought everything back into question.

"So you mean it wasn't Julien who...?"

"Your wife's brother? Good lord no, that poor soul had absolutely nothing to do with it. The man in question is a colleague of Elsa's. Can you believe it? He'd locked her up in his shop's storeroom."

"Wait, someone called Paul?" I ventured.

"Spot on. A total psychopath, you can see it as soon as you clap eyes on him. To put you in the picture it's thanks to your witness statements that we found him so quickly. You'd said that two messages had been sent from Elsa's phone. After we'd checked, it was confirmed that the one had indeed been sent to Julien. On the other hand, there was no trace found of that other message allegedly sent, which our friend Paul would've received. That's what got our attention. It was that one extra lie that made him stand out. So we paid him a little visit, which really paid off."

"Did he say why he did it?"

"To put you in the picture, he came clean straight away. He'd fallen for Elsa's charms quite some time ago, something that was in no way reciprocated by her I can assure you. When Elsa told him that she was hoping to marry Julien, he went crazy. He couldn't think of anything else to do, but to lock her up in the basement of the shop. I have to say he wasn't thinking clearly at that time. Once his compulsion had subsided, he realised he didn't know what to do. He couldn't just let her go as if nothing had happened, but he didn't want to do her any harm either. He kept her locked up until we found her, bringing her something to eat but threatening her just enough so she didn't make any noise. No one working there would have suspected a thing. To put you in the picture, that cellar is a really isolated place, you get to it through the back of the shop."

I shuddered at the idea of Elsa being just a few metres from where we had been standing when we went to that shop. As for the guilty party, I would have preferred that it was his other colleague Marthe, who'd been so unwelcoming to us. It was such a shame. I was relieved in any case to know that Julien was innocent, even if I couldn't boast that I'd believed in him right from the start. Superintendent Colin couldn't either. I thought I was above all outside influences and jumping to hasty conclusions. My brave denouncing of him had suddenly looked much more like a vile act of whistle-blowing.

I pushed open the glass door and told a stunned audience of the happy outcome, taking great care not to linger on our suspicions of Julien or on our trip to Paris.

"Louis there's something I just don't quite get." Julien asked me after my story was over.

"Five minutes ago you went off to call a customer and now you're telling me you've just spoken to the cops."

The silence that followed was to say the least somewhat embarrassing. We were all staring at each other.

One thing had to come out of this and that was to appear as the receiver of the call and in no way its maker. I could very easily have had an incoming call while speaking to my customer; there was no need to make a huge deal about it. I cleared my throat so I could get my answer out better, but Maxime saw fit to interrupt me at that precise moment.

"Well you know, we all thought you were on the run, even your own sister thought so!"

The silence that followed was even more unbearable than the first one. Delphine's brother eventually got up with a huge smile on his face.

"Oh you old fool you!" he exclaimed while giving Maxime and enormous slap on the back. Maxime had just been on the receiving end of Alice nudging him violently in his side while I was kicking him hard in the shins under the table.

However, when the name of Elsa's colleague Paul was brought up again, he soon lost his happy face.

"Someone will pay. I swear I'll kill him!"

Epilogue

"Louis, are you ready? We're late!"

"You'll laugh. I can't get into my suit anymore!"

I'd acquired new expertise in obtaining richer and richer customers. I'd gained a real taste for the high life and all the little treats that go with it. It was practical and beneficial to my wallet, but much less so for my waistline.

On this particular day, Delphine and I were expected at an altogether different type of event, Julien and Elsa's marriage. A year had passed since the drama had unfolded, which shook the couple to their core. We'd got to know Elsa, a wonderful young lady, who'd managed to instil in Julien some good manners. She'd gradually recovered from her ordeal and even seemed, unlike her future husband, to have forgiven Paul for his misdeeds. Paul's time in prison had been commuted to a spell in a psychiatric hospital. Paul was suffering from bipolar disorder whose attacks although infrequent could achieve an alarmingly high frequency. Until then his sickness had never been taken seriously, but it fitted in well with the witness statements made by his colleagues about his everyday behaviour.

Before his arrest, Paul had held the manager's position. This job was naturally given to Elsa. She is equally capable in her management skills as she is in her decision-making skills. Elsa had breathed new life into the shop by upping the range and authenticity of the goods on offer to her customers. I'd even offered my skills by helping out with some renovation work.

As a result of the good business, the couple had been able to arrange their dream marriage. They'd hired a wonderfully restored former convent and had sent out a really wide range of invitations to the wedding.

During the reception, I noticed Superintendent Colin dancing away arm in arm with a strongly built woman on the dance floor waving his goatee around wildly. The woman seemed somewhat familiar to me.

"Marthe, well I'll be!" I whispered to Julien, who was standing next to me. "The last time I saw her she was in no hurry to shift her bustle."

"She totally changed once she'd left her husband and found a much better match!"

I had to clear my mind for a little while, so I could really take on board this bizarre scene I saw before me.

"And this match is…"

"Yes it is Superintendent Colin." said Julien.

"That's huge… the coincidence I mean!"

"It's no coincidence. They saw each other for many hours during the inquiry period following Paul's arrest. It was love at first sight!"

Even though it seemed like, all's well that ends well, without knowing quite why, all this success had made me feel ill at ease. Julien, who seemed to be thinking what I was thinking, knew exactly what to say at that exact moment.

"We should raise a toast to Paul, because, after all is said and done, we owe him a great deal."

9 791094 170038